Farmer George
and the Fieldmice

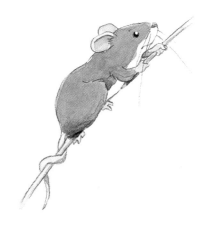

Farmer George
and the Fieldmice

Nick Ward

PAVILION

First published in Great Britain in 1999 by
PAVILION BOOKS LIMITED
London House, Great Eastern Wharf
Parkgate Road, London SW11 4NQ

Text and illustrations © Nick Ward

The moral right of the author and illustrator
has been asserted

Designed by Ness Wood at Zoom Design

A CIP catalogue record for this book is available
from the British Library.

ISBN 1 86205 203 4

Set in Bell MT
Printed in Singapore by Imago
Colour origination in Hong Kong by Asia Graphic Output

2 4 6 8 10 9 7 5 3 1

This book can be ordered direct from the publisher. Please contact
the Marketing Department. But try your bookshop first.

Farmer George looked out of his
window. It was a glorious summer's day.
"Perfect," smiled Farmer George.
"Time to harvest the wheat."
He filled his flask with orange and
wrapped some sandwiches for lunch.

Farmer George marched
across the lane to the wheat field.
"Yap!" barked Tam.

"Sorry boy," called Farmer George. "You stay and look after the farm." He opened the gate and disappeared inside a dark, rickety shed.

Brrum! Out he drove on a shiny new combine harvester. Chug, chug, rumble! Up the field and back again, the combine sliced a great swathe of corn.

Farmer George breathed in the warm summer air. He loved harvest time. Out in the field, all on his own. But…

…Somewhere deep in the stalks of wheat, a family of fieldmice were snoring gently in their nest, when… chug, chug, rumble! The fieldmice woke with a start. What was that terrible noise?

Mrs Fieldmouse rushed to the top of a stalk of wheat. Oh dear! It was Farmer George driving his noisy red combine, chopping down the wheat.

"Stop," squeaked Mrs Fieldmouse, but of course Farmer George couldn't hear her. She must stop him. But how? Tam was clever. Tam would know!

"Take the children to safety," she told her husband "I'll be right back."

And off she scampered, across the field…

through the
hedge… and
over the lane.
The combine
rumbled on.

Tam was dozing by the farm gate.
"Tam!" Mrs Fieldmouse gasped.
"Help me please!" Tam listened,
gave a single yap
and raced into
the farmyard.

A minute later Tam returned…
followed by Prudence,
Woolly and Rooster,
Farmer George's biggest
and noisiest cockerel.

"Listen," barked Tam. "This is what we must do…"

Mr Fieldmouse and the children watched helplessly from the edge of the field, as the combine thundered on, straight towards their home. Closer and closer and closer.

"Hurry up Mrs Fieldmouse, hurry up Tam," they squealed.

"Quickly," puffed Mrs Fieldmouse, "We haven't much time." The rescuers charged through the wheat, until they reached the nest.

"Now!" yapped Tam. Quick as a flash, Woolly jumped up onto Prudence's back. Tam leapt onto Woolly and Rooster perched on top of Tam's head.

"Cocka-doodle-doo," he yelled…

Farmer George jumped in alarm. What was that? And then he saw, right out in front of him, Rooster and Tam peeking between the ears of wheat!

He yanked on the brake and the combine wheezed to a halt.

"What's the matter?" asked Farmer George, rushing over to the animals. "Yap," barked Tam. "Yap, yap!"

Farmer George bent down and carefully parted the stalks. "Oh, I see," he smiled. "Well done! But don't worry, I know just what to do."

What did Farmer George do? Well, he finished cutting the wheat…

…all except the small clump where the fieldmice had their nest. With some string, some wood and a bright blue ribbon, he made their home as safe and cosy as could be!

When he had finished, Farmer George remembered his lunch. "Goodness, I'm hungry," he said.

So as the sun started to
sink in the great, wide sky,
they sat by the oak tree and
Farmer George shared his
sandwiches with his friends.

Why not trace and colour in some of your own pictures of Farmer George and his animals?

Farmer George

Tam
the Dog

Mrs Fieldmouse

Woolly
the Sheep